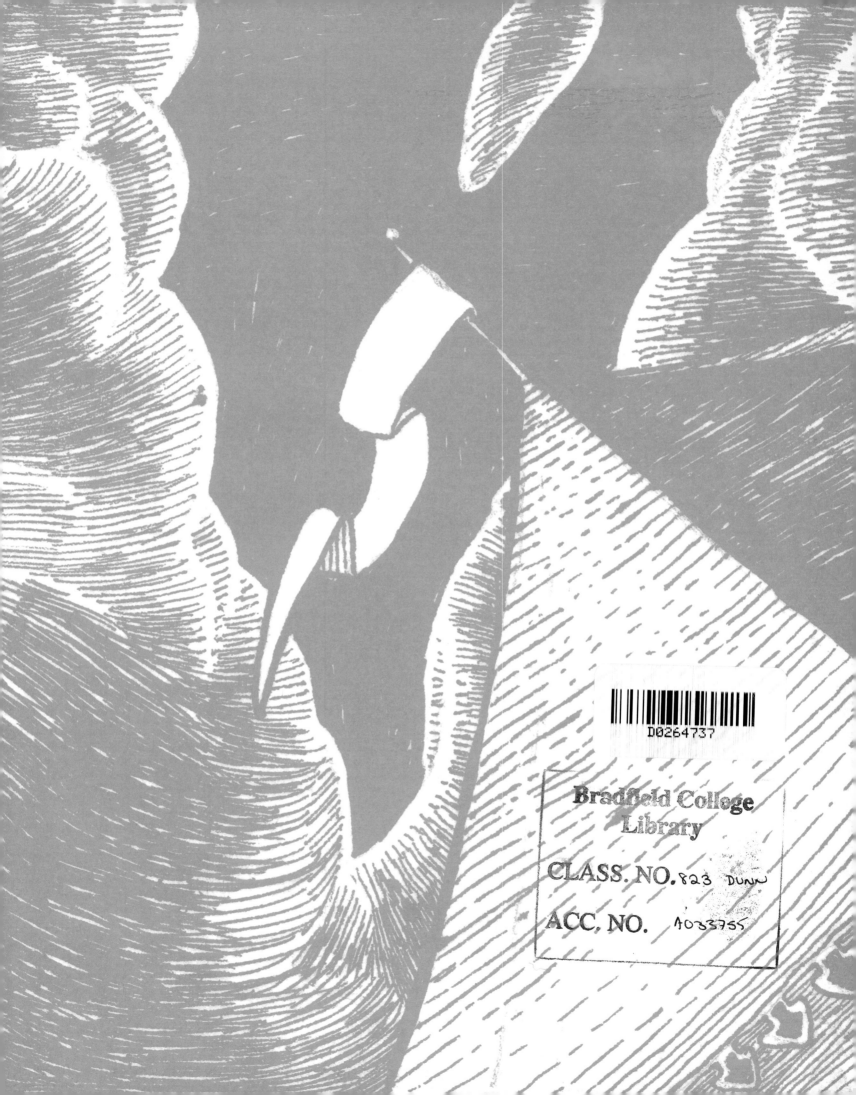

D0264737

Bradfield College
Library

CLASS. NO. 823 DUNN

ACC. NO. 4033755

"A wonderfully imaginative and stylish piece of work and a perfect example of the adventurous new directions that comic books should be taking in the future."
Alan Moore, author of *Watchmen* and *V for Vendetta*

"*Salem Brownstone* is a hypnotically beautiful gothic fantasy."
Jefferson Hack,
Dazed & Confused

"*Salem Brownstone* kicked my ass and made me believe in the beautiful darkness of the world again."
Harmony Korine, screenplay writer of *Kids* and director of *Gummo*

"*Salem Brownstone* is a graphic novel that is both original and compelling. There's a seamless relationship between the images and the text, and the characters linger in the mind."
Anthony Minghella, director of *The Talented Mr Ripley* and *The English Patient*

"Our new century demands a new charismatic comic-book magician to weave his spells on us. Updating classic conjurors like Mandrake and Doctor Strange with a twist of Oscar Wilde and Aubrey Beardsley, John Dunning and Nikhil Singh have crafted a haunting, hypnotising master of the mystic arts in *Salem Brownstone*. Their sharp, surprising storytelling and intense, imaginative illustration combine to create real magic on the page."
Paul Gravett, author of *Graphic Novels: Stories to Change Your Life* and director of the Comica Festival in London

There are those who love the rum and unusual, the uncanny, the macabre. Perhaps they wish for thrilling horrors in their own seemingly mundane lives... But they should beware what they wish for.

Take Salem Brownstone, for instance. For many years he ran the Sit & Spin Laundromat and was content with his lot. The Laundromat was his own fiefdom, and the customers presented him with a never-ending cavalcade of variety. And yet, somewhere deep down Salem believed he was destined for greater things, stranger things. Then one day they came to him in the unlikely form of a simple telegram...

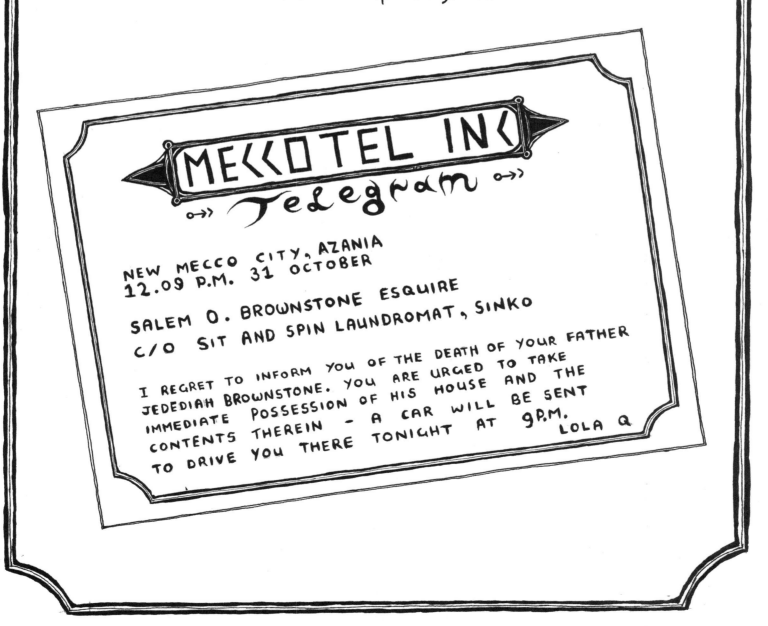

MECCOTEL INC
Telegram

NEW MECCO CITY, AZANIA
12.09 P.M. 31 OCTOBER

SALEM O. BROWNSTONE ESQUIRE
C/O SIT AND SPIN LAUNDROMAT, SINKO

I REGRET TO INFORM YOU OF THE DEATH OF YOUR FATHER JEDEDIAH BROWNSTONE. YOU ARE URGED TO TAKE IMMEDIATE POSSESSION OF HIS HOUSE AND THE CONTENTS THEREIN - A CAR WILL BE SENT TO DRIVE YOU THERE TONIGHT AT 9P.M.
LOLA Q

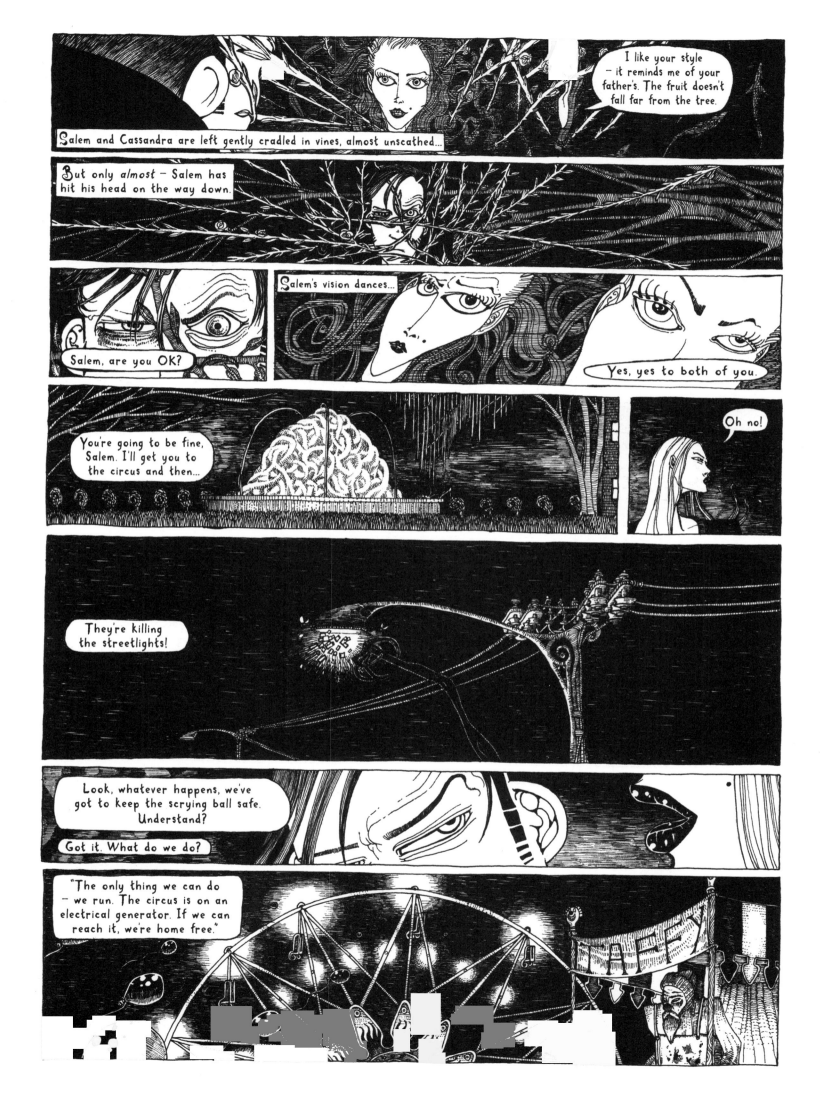

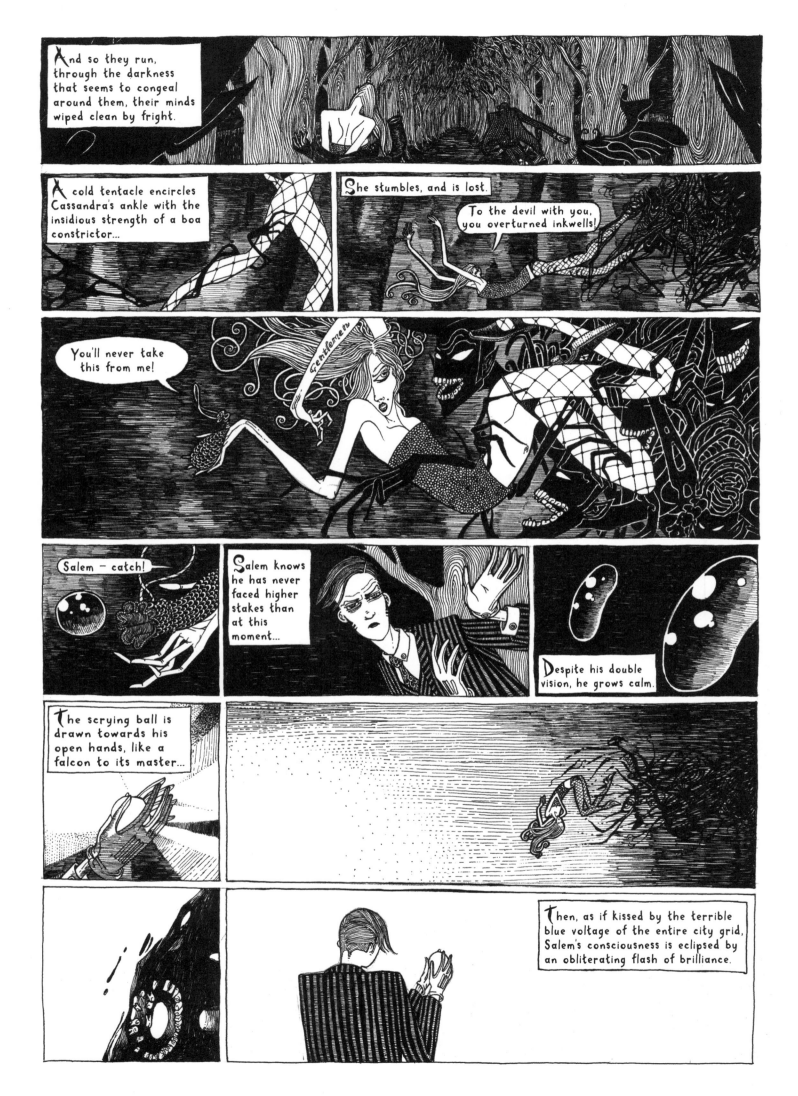

His mind bucks, then is free of its physical confines: a mote in the eye of God.

Salem is aware of his body, his name, his life, drifting somewhere far below. A sudden contraction of fear threatens to overwhelm him...

Then he is aware that he is not alone, and is comforted.

The smell of popcorn, sawdust and burned candyfloss can only mean...

THE CIRCUS!

Here, all that is ordinary is useless. Only the extraordinary survive...

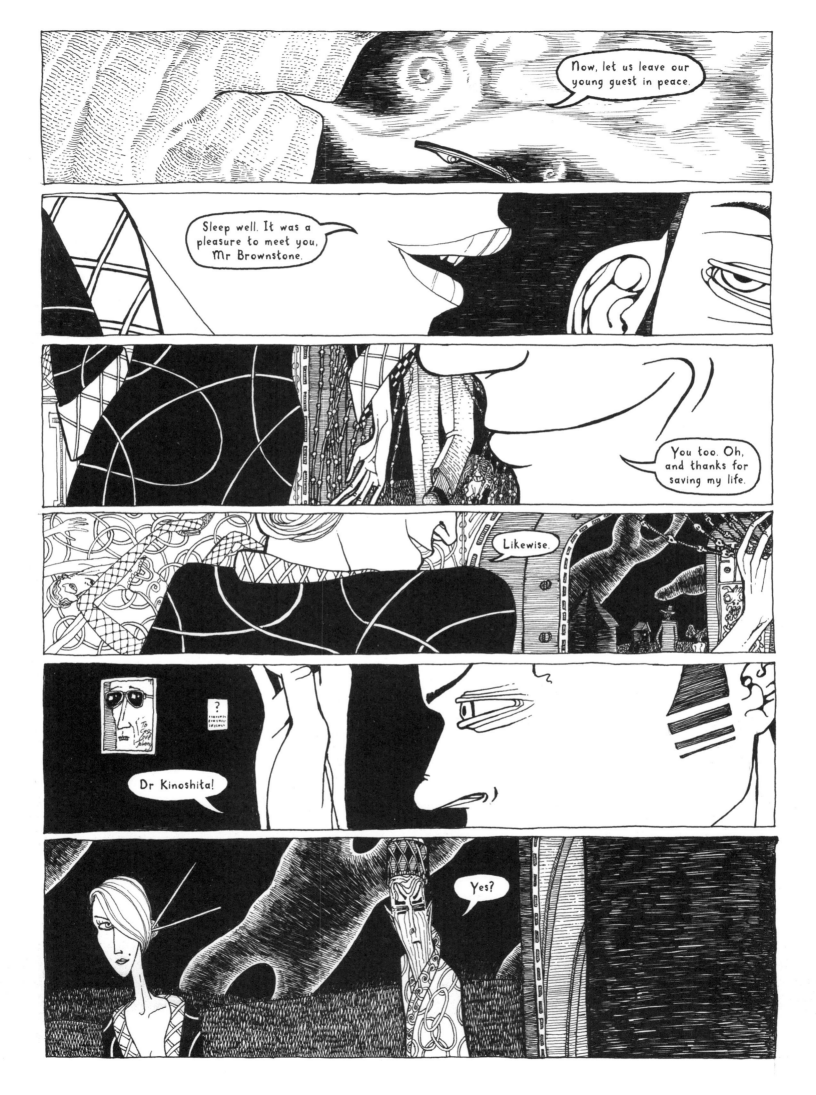

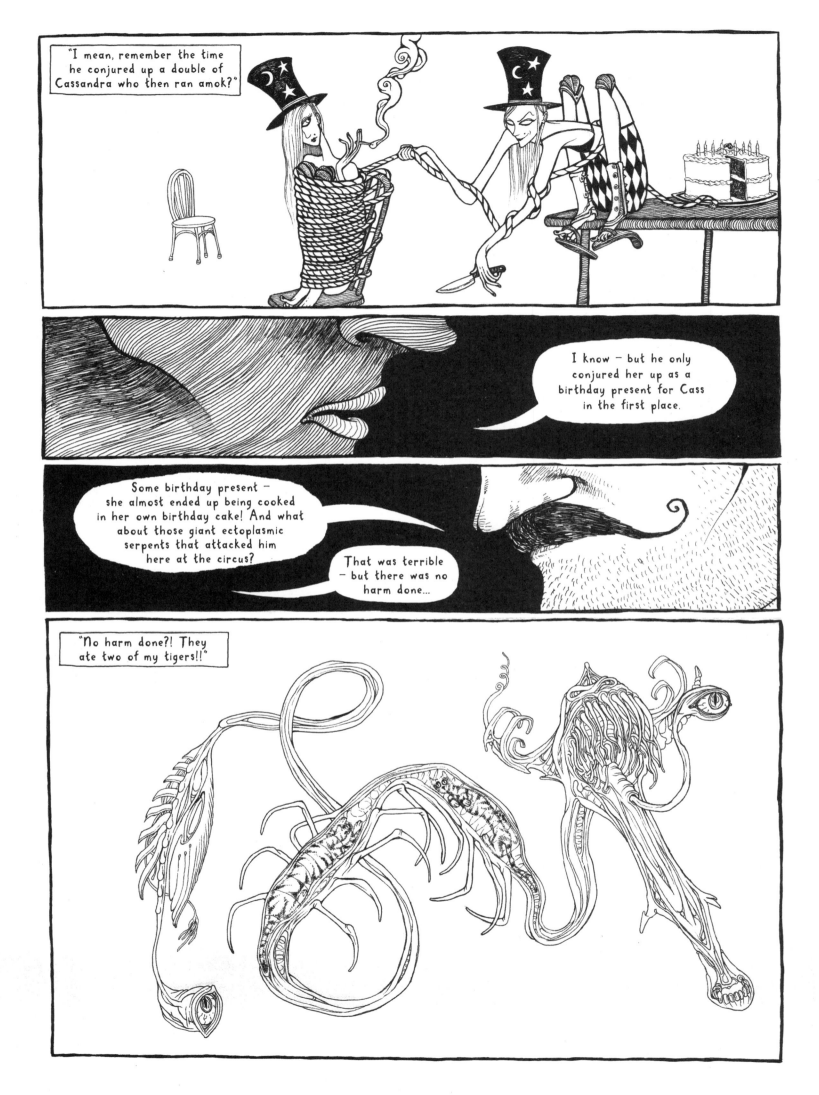

M eanwhile,
smoke hangs over the
Brownstone manse...

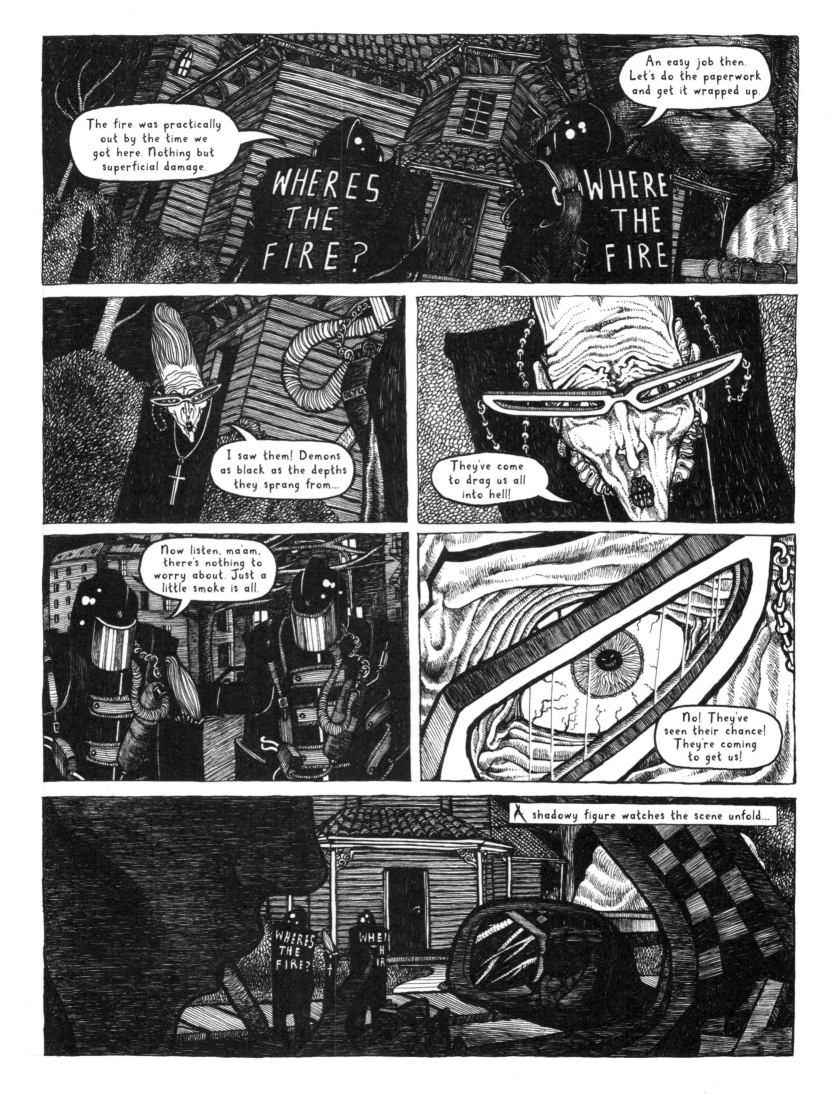

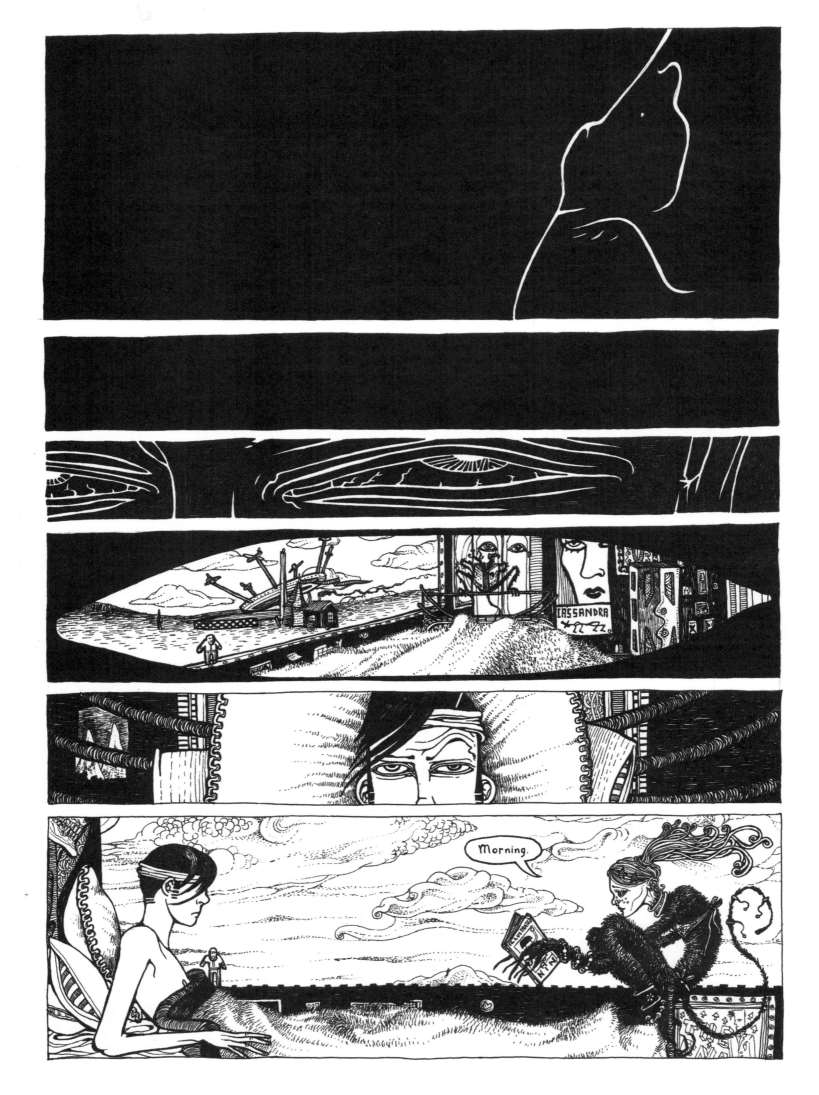

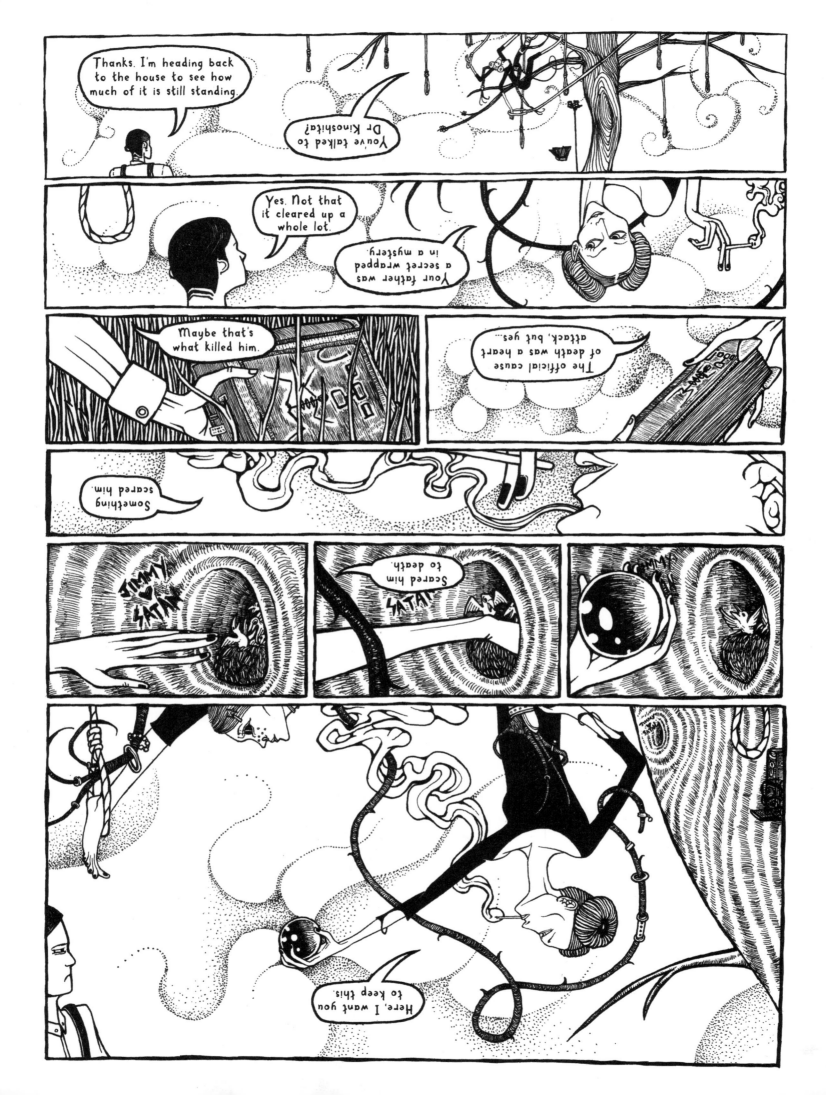

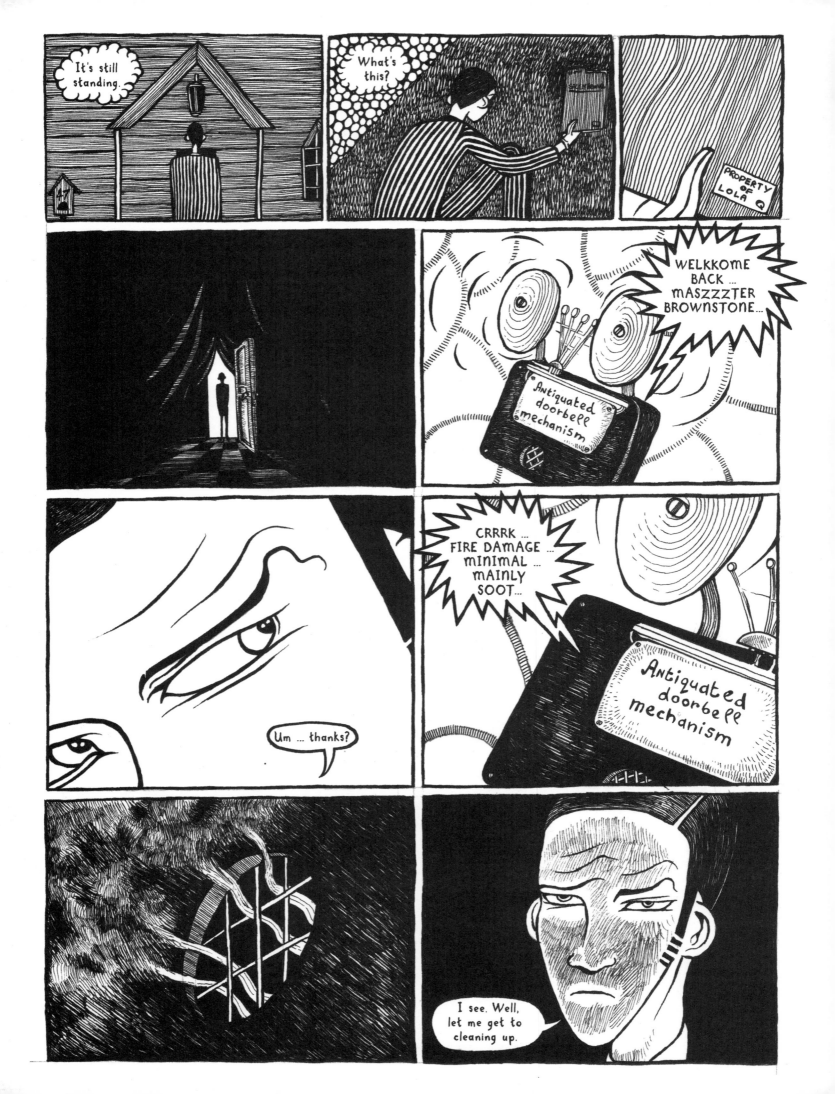

In another place...

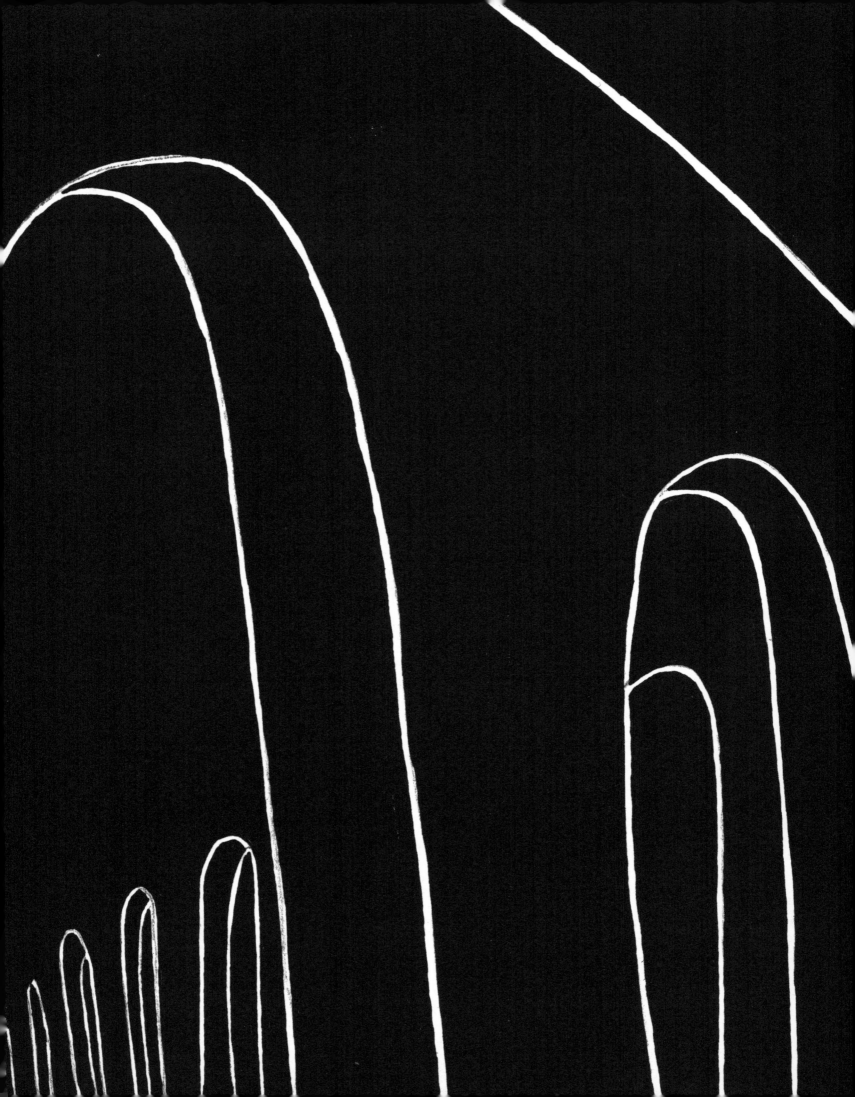

...lies Mu' bric,
the Midnight City...

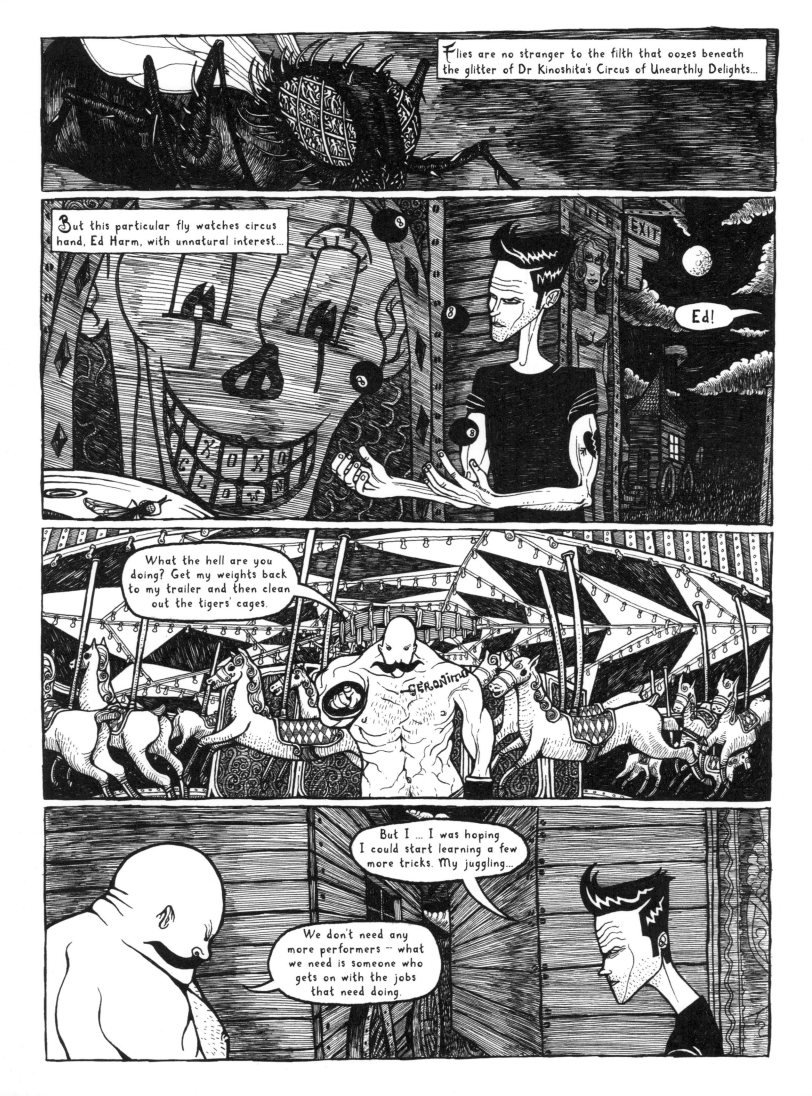

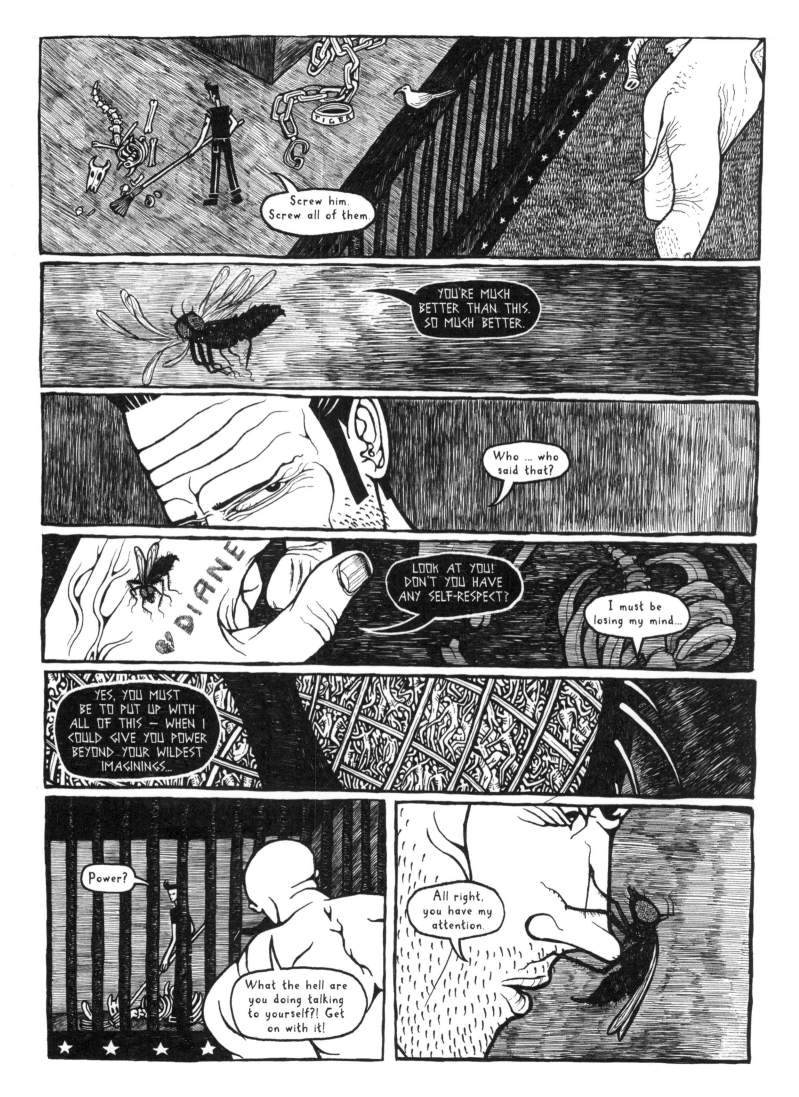

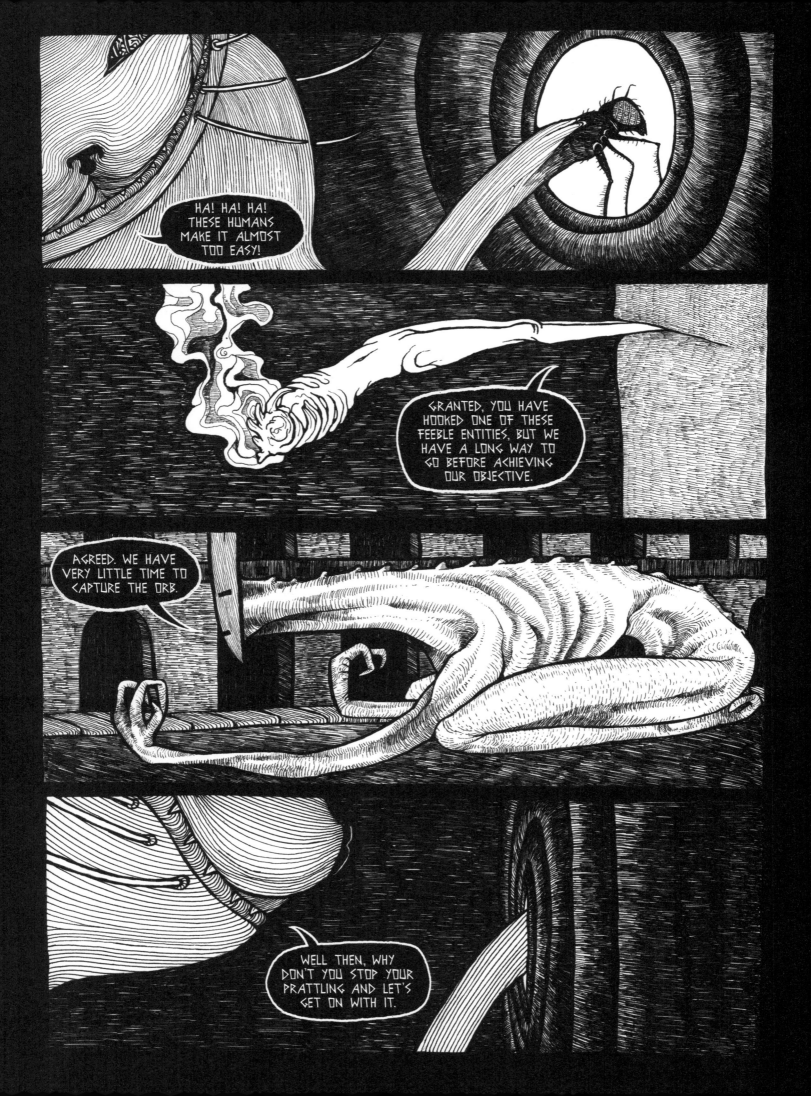

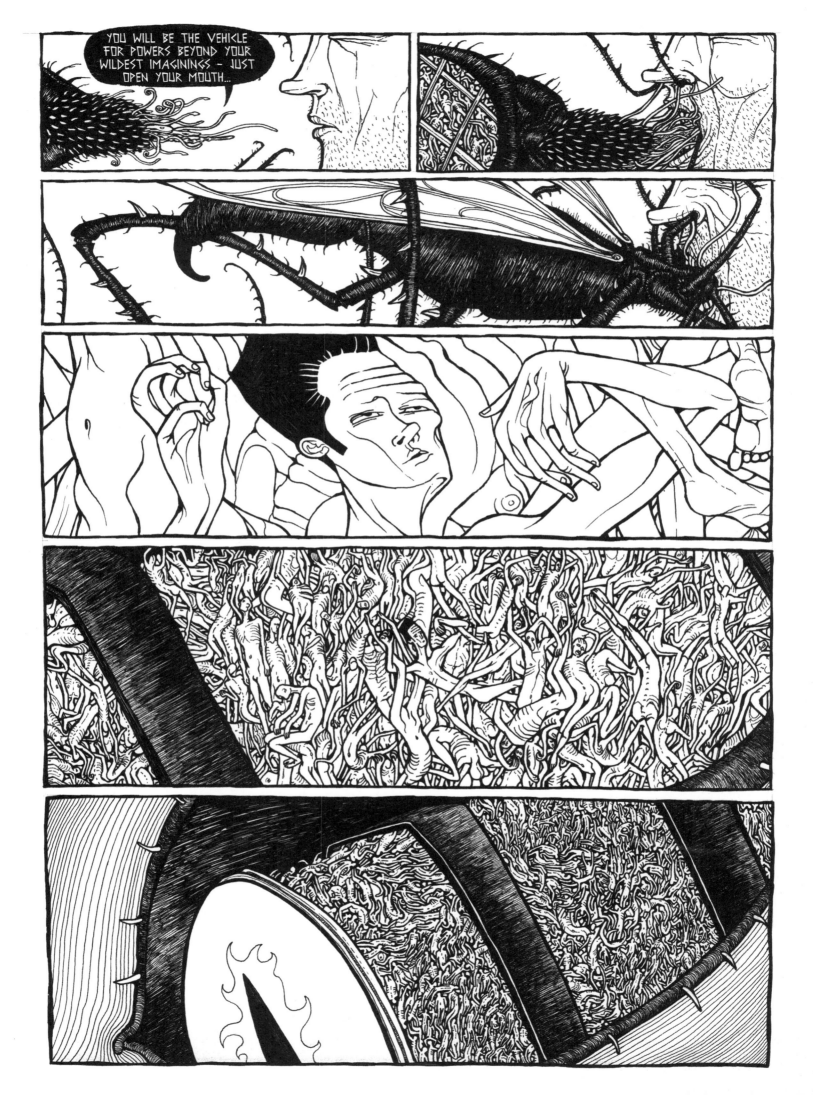

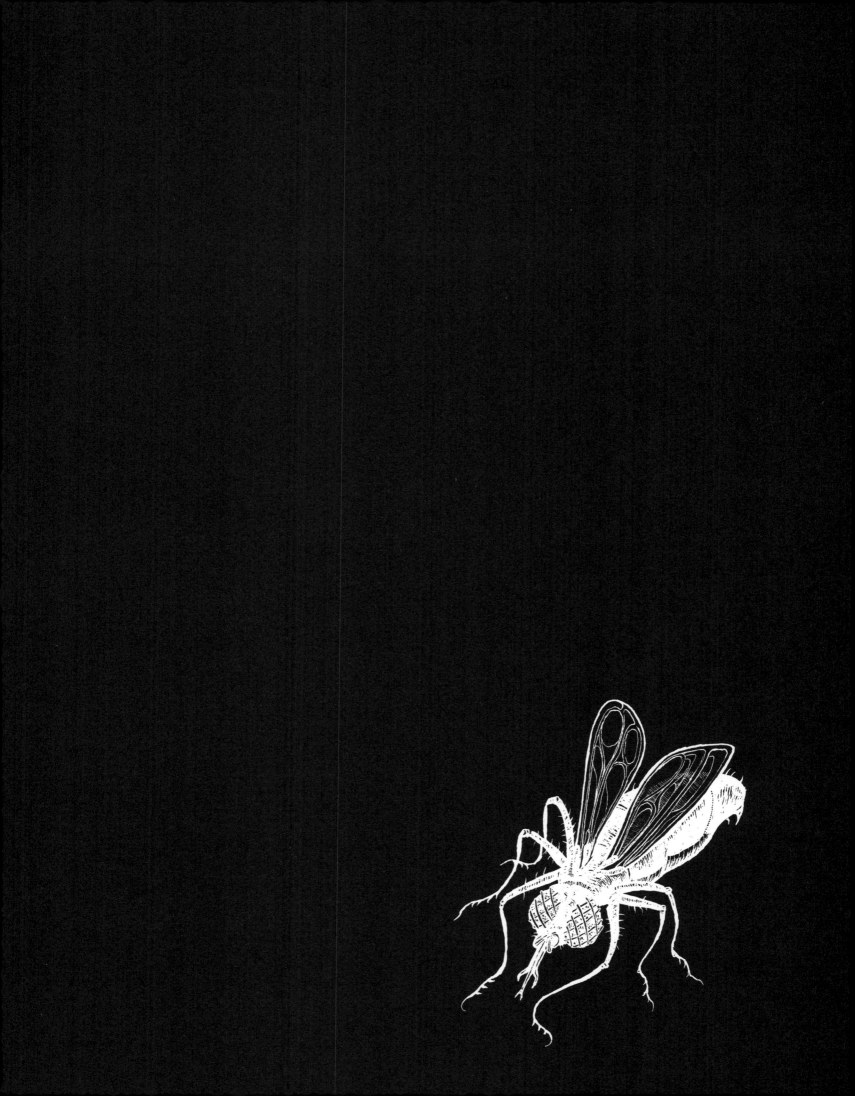

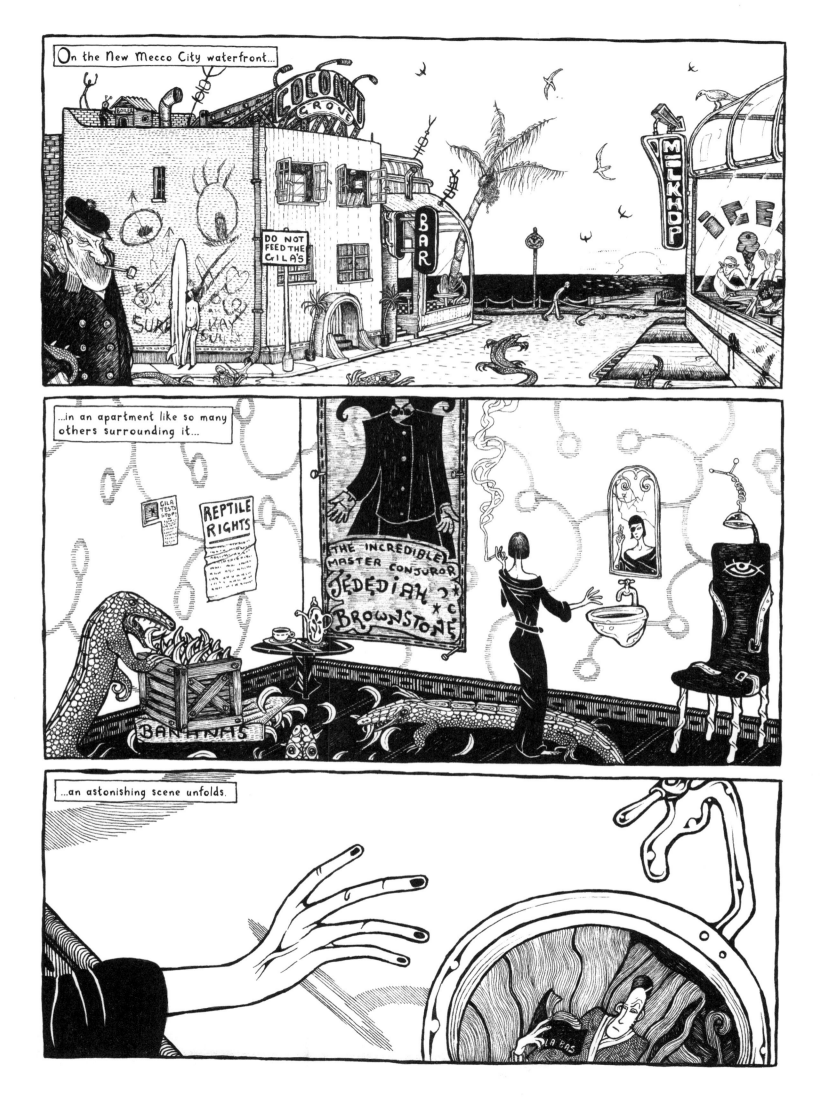

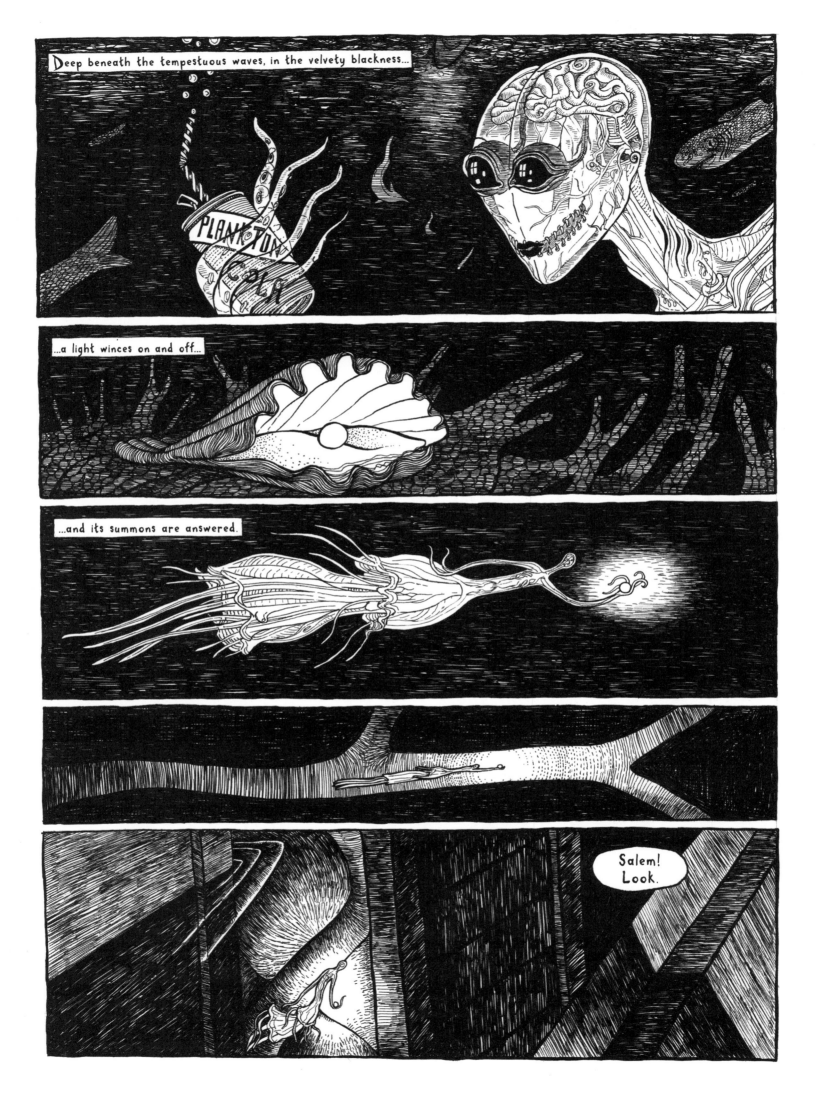

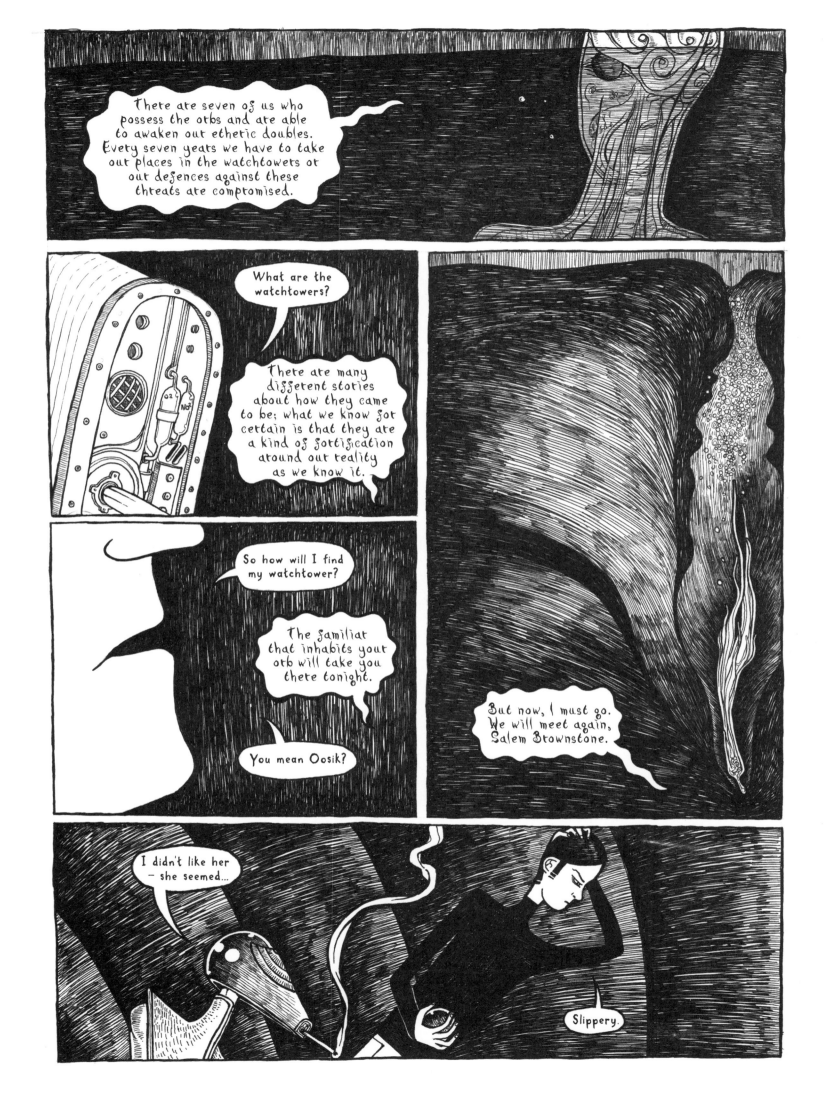

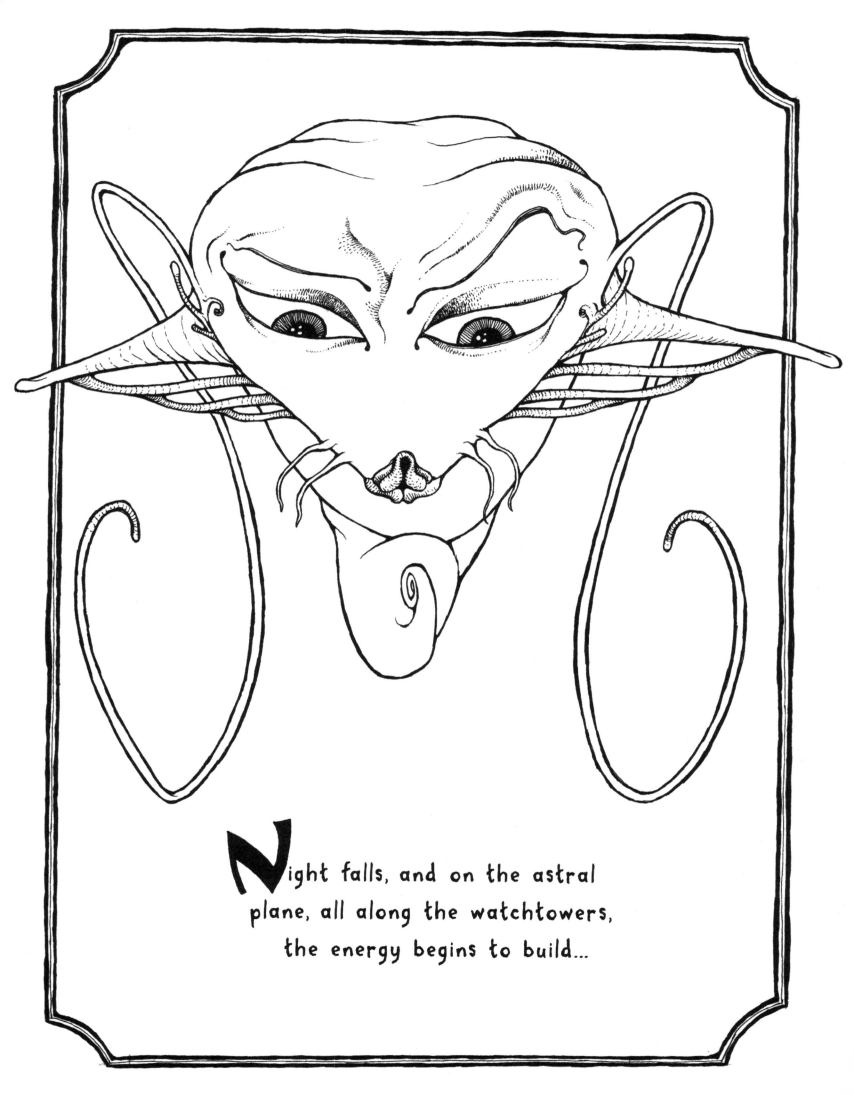

Night falls, and on the astral
plane, all along the watchtowers,
the energy begins to build...

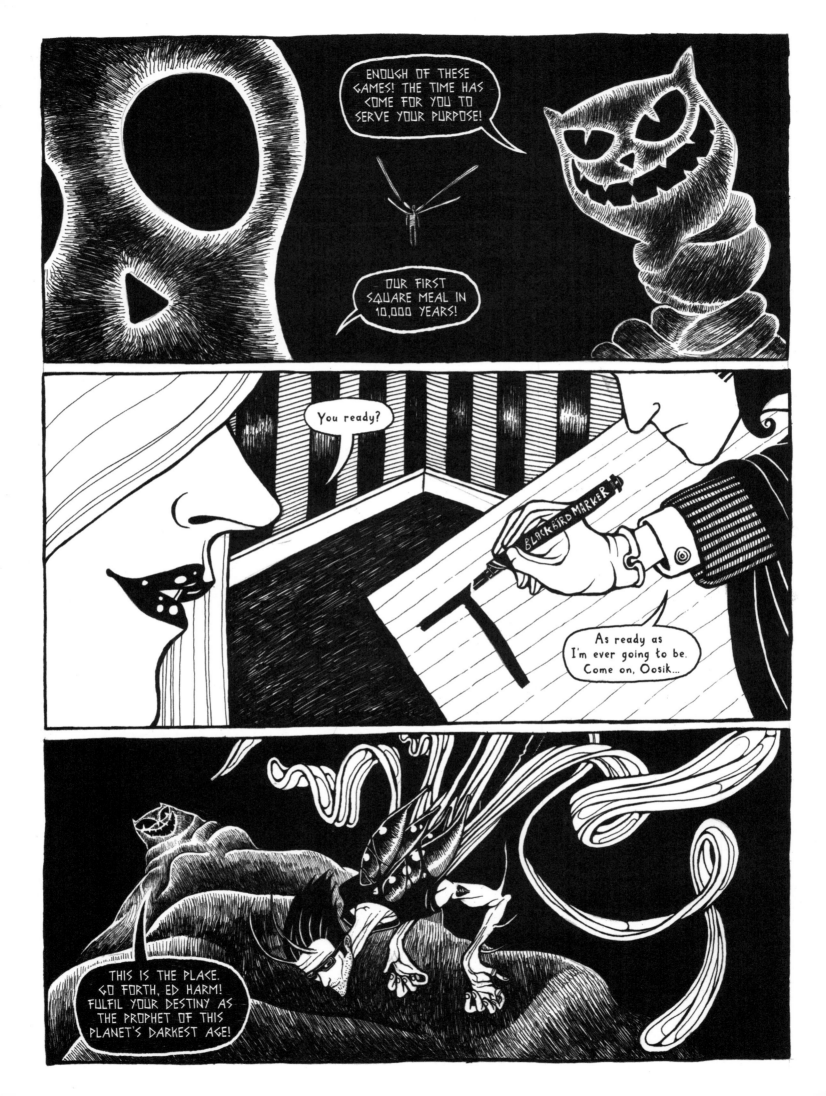

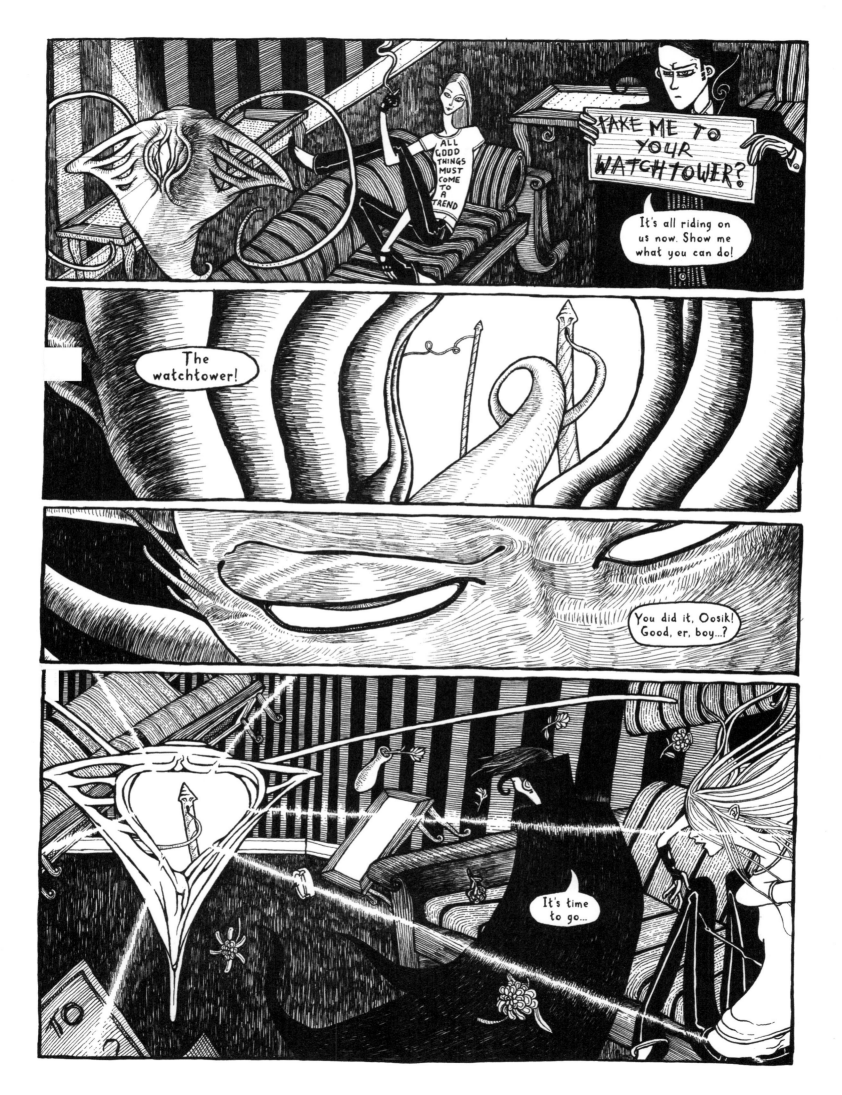

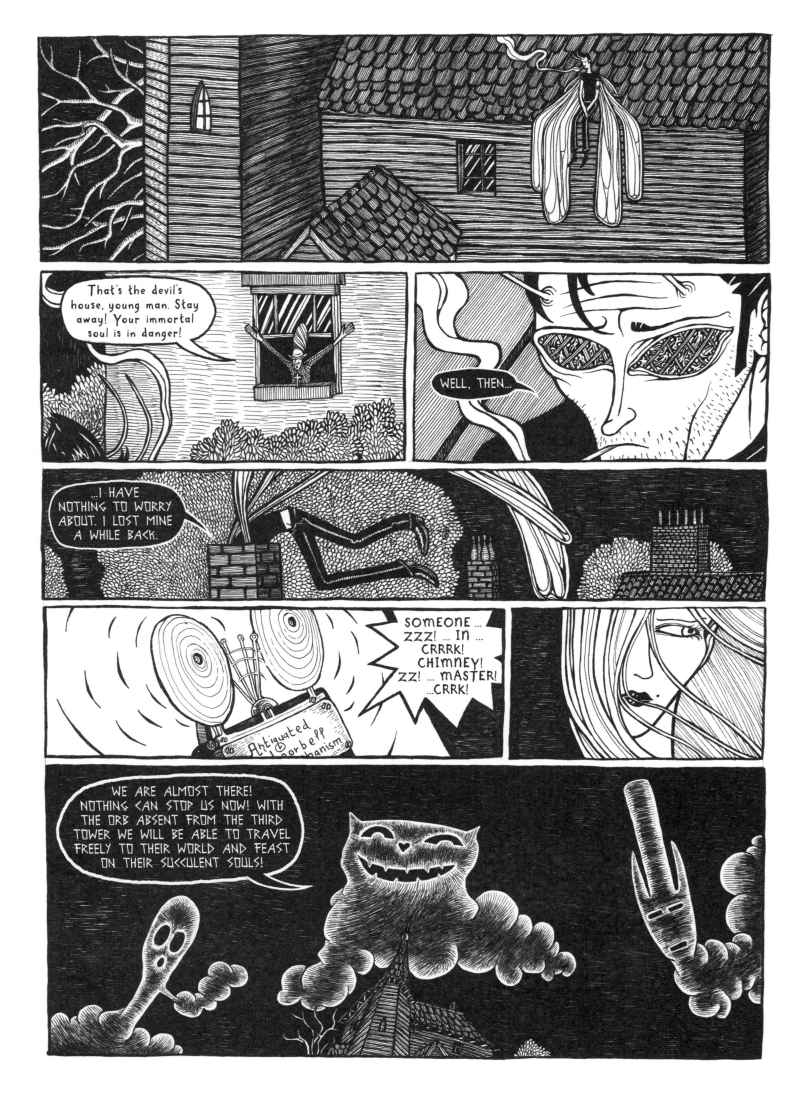

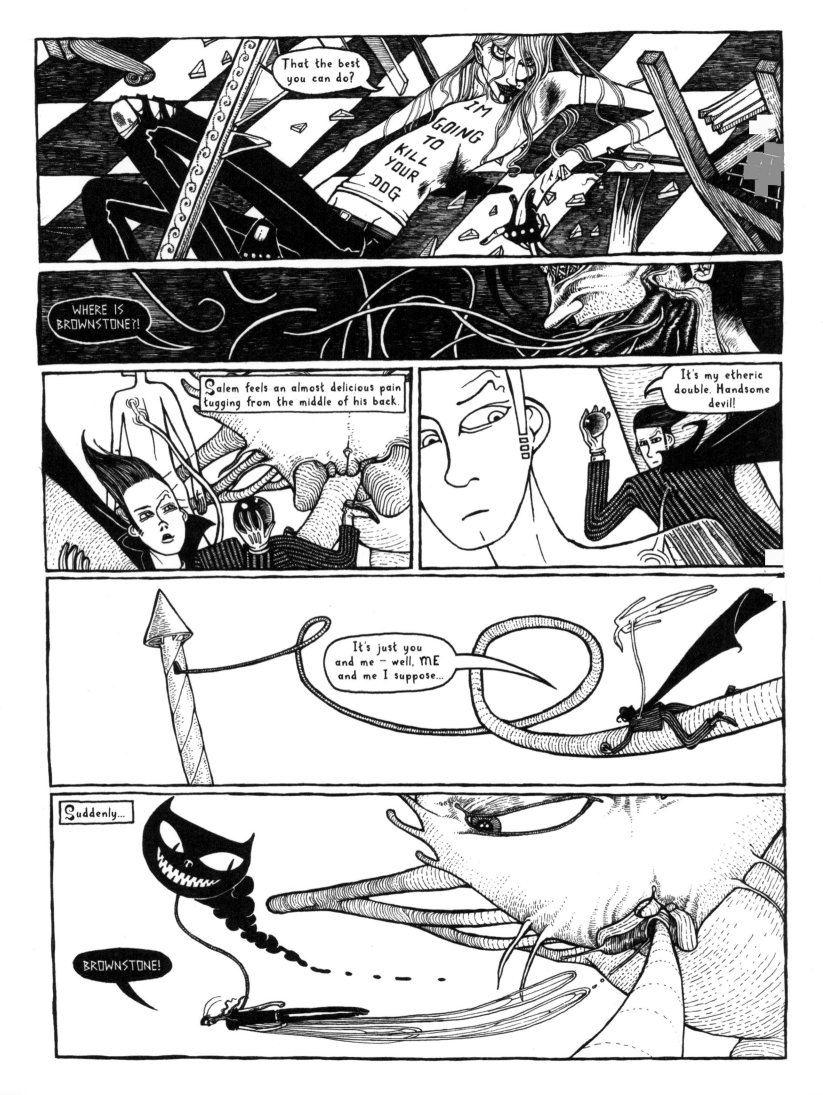

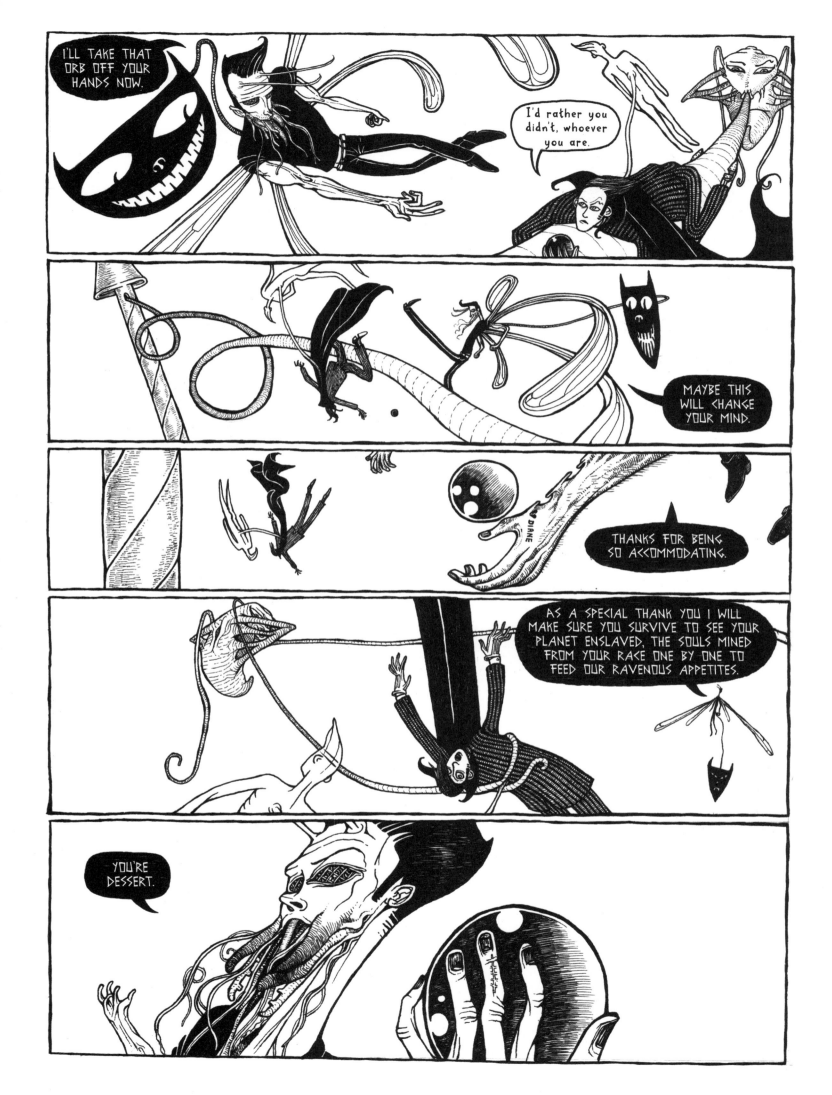

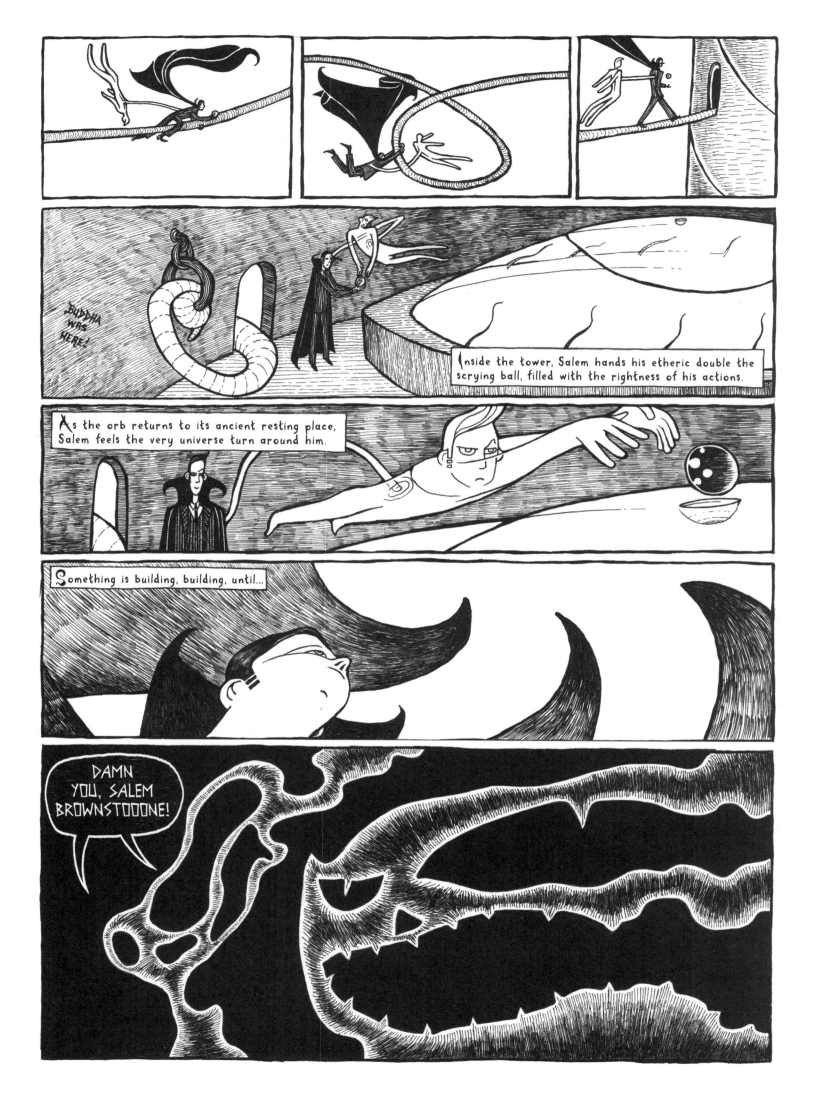

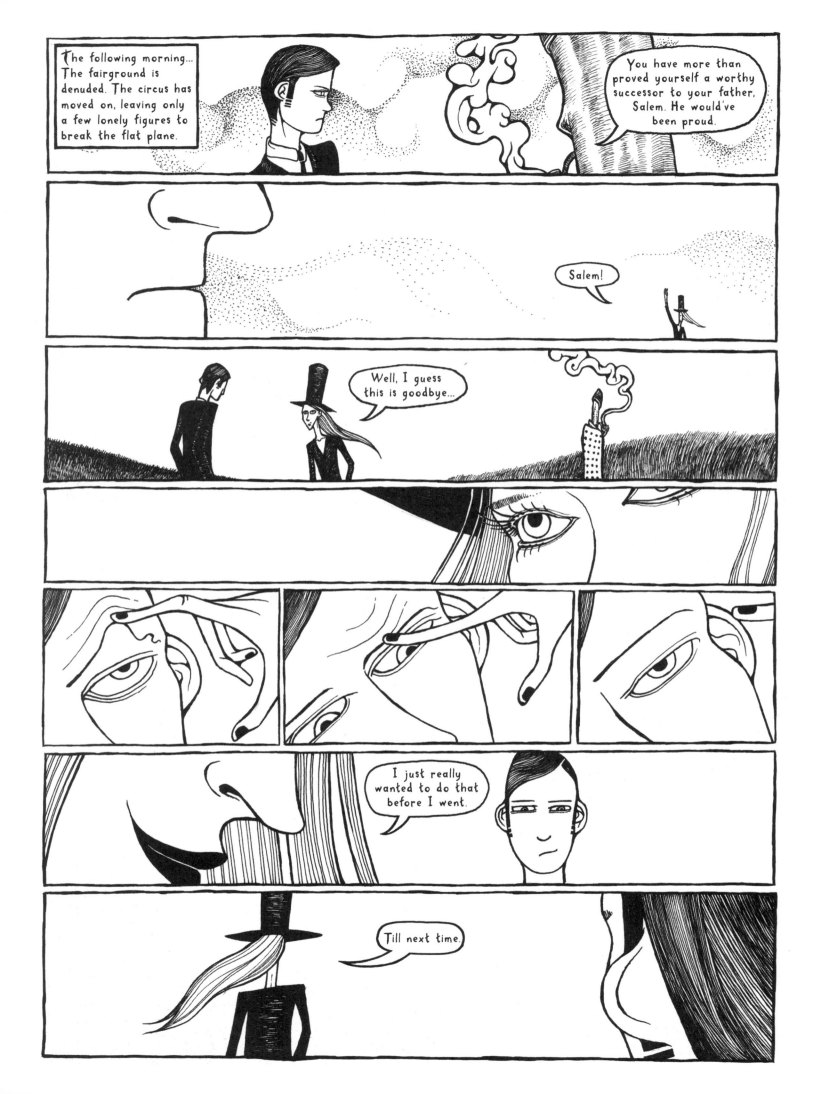

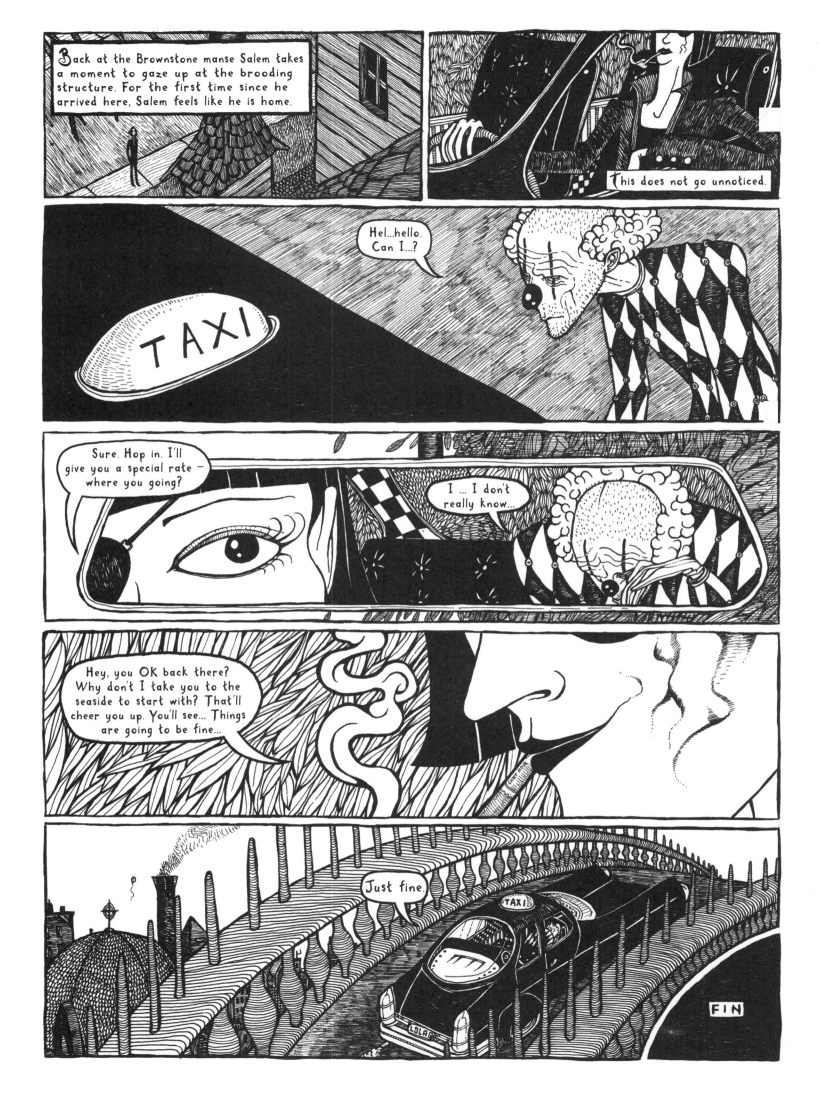

THE DARK
ELDERS OF
MU'BRIC

ED HARM

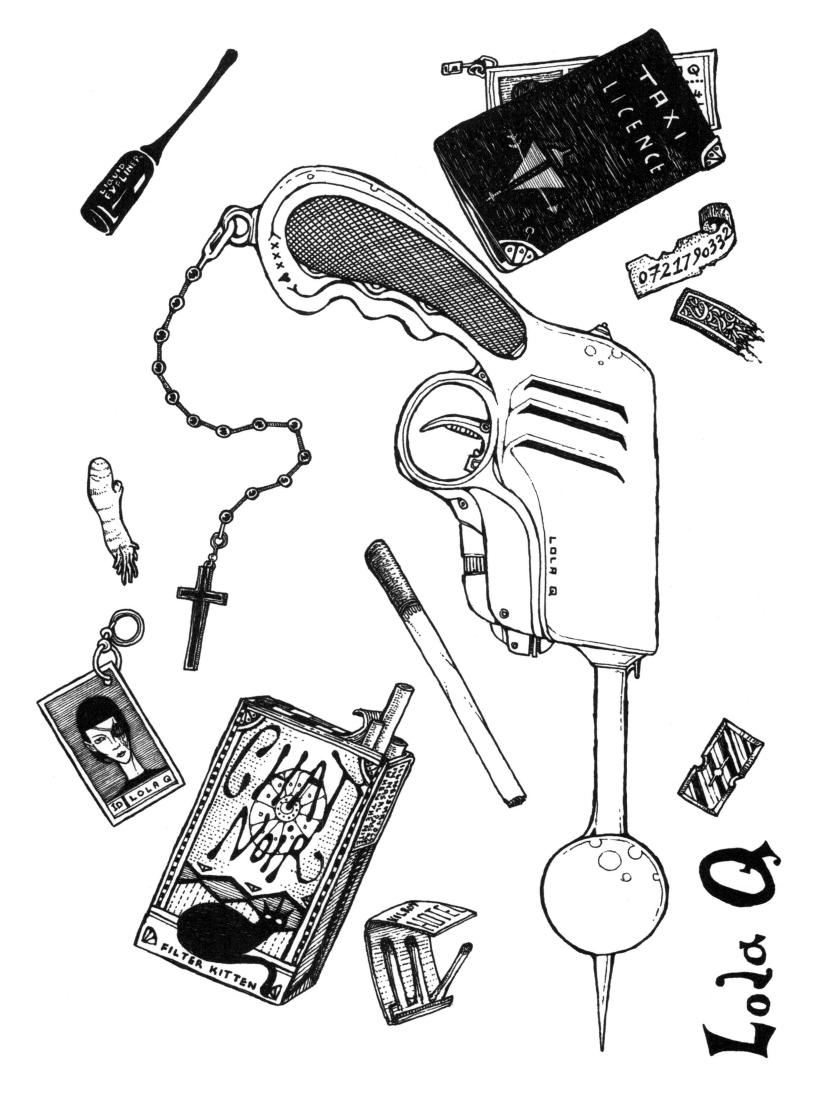

salem brownstone

would like to thank his uncle Paul Gravett, his godparents Simon Davis and Sylvia Farago, Jefferson Hack, Patrick Insole, Harmony Korine, Fiona McMorrough, Anthony Minghella, Jon Morgan, Mark Sinclair, Lizzie Spratt & Sarah Such.
Abracadabra!

✷ ✷ ✷

john harris dunning

This book is dedicated to Peter Watson, for all your love and support.

I'd like to thank my parents Carol and Simon Dunning, my sister Georgia Morris, and the rest of my family. The encouragement of my friends has been invaluable, especially that of Craig Bregman, Alex De Campi, Christian De Sousa, Lisa Cohn, Roland Erasmus, Jo Hebouche, Richard James, Lara Lombaard, Sacha Mardou, Mark Pool & Rory Stead.

Big up to the Midwich Cuckoos: Dylan, Imogen and Abigail Morris, Esmé & Milo Davis, Lucas & Max Abelson, Silva De Sousa, Alexander, Daniel & Thomas Fives, Saffron, Hannah and Amina Hebouche, Fynn Oldreive, Milo & Hela Watson & Harvey Yeomans.

✷ ✷ ✷

John Harris Dunning was born in Zululand, South Africa. He now lives in Hampstead, London's most haunted suburb.

Visit: www.tibet-foundation.org

nikhil singh

Salem was drawn sporadically over a period of seven years. Consequently, I am obliged to thank a lot of people whose help and assistance was both vital and invaluable.

The first half drawn at the Daily Deli, 13 Brownlow, Cape Town.
The second half at 10 Kidderpore Gardens, Hampstead.

CAPE TOWN
Thanks to Melanie for being a guiding light and for showing me how to build the pyramid. Thanks to Angelika for the fireside freakouts – they helped! Thanks to Sinead for keeping me on track. Thanks to Bona for being a sibling. Thanks to Cass for the psychic hotline. Thanks to Elise for the mermaids. Thanks to Gareth for finding the frequency. Thanks to Len for defending humanity. And thanks to Jemstone for always grounding me in the universe.

HAMPSTEAD
Thanks to Pekka for unimaginable support and unshakeable faith in rock and roll. Thanks to Simon Psi the all-seeing eye. Thanks to Alain for popping a cap in Satan's Nazi ass. Thanks to Juan-Erh for the plot on the Orient Express. Thanks to my mom for being a good friend. Thanks to Talitha for the dreams in the doll's house. And special thanks to Carmen, Empress of the two White Cats, for keeping me alive in deep space, guarding the gate to fairyland and riding the wild white unicorns.

✷ ✷ ✷

Witchboy. Were-cat. High ranking member of the Venusian Secret Service. Nikhil left school at 16 and has undergone no formal draining at any institutes of higher burning. He currently lives in an ivory tower and is never coming back to your planet EVER AGAIN.

Visit his grave at www.nikhilsingh.com